Moody

Benchmark Books
Marshall Cavendish Corporation
99 White Plains Road
Tarrytown, New York 10591-9001

Series created by AS Publishing

Library of Congress Cataloging-in-Publication Data

Amos, Janine.
      Moody / by Janine Amos : illustrated by Gwen Green.
         p. cm. – (It's your choice)
      Summary: A story about a girl who starts to feel bad
when she is away from her mother for the first time
provides questions for a discussion of moods.
      ISBN 0-7614-0099-0 (lib, bdg.).
      1.Mood (Psychology) – Juvenile literature. [1. Mood
(Psychology)] I.Green, Gwen, ill. II. Title. III. Series:
Amos, Janine. It's your choice.
BF521.A46 1995
152.4 – dc20   95-4299
                                                CIP
                                                AC

Printed in Hong Kong by Imago Publishing Ltd.
Bound in the USA

Moody

By Janine Amos
Illustrated by Gwen Green

BENCHMARK BOOKS

Maya's story

Maya looked out of the car window. She could see some tents. They must be nearly at the campsite! Maya was excited. She was on vacation with her cousins. It was her first time without her mom and dad.

Maya's Aunty Cass parked the car. Donna, Leroy and Ben swung open the doors. They rushed to the trunk and started to unpack.

"Let's play football!" said Ben, bouncing his new ball.

"Let's eat first – I'm starving!" said Leroy.

Donna pulled out her camera. "I'll take a picture of us all," she said. "Smile!"

"Come on, Maya!" called Aunty Cass. "Come and be in the photo!"

Maya ran over and joined in. She gave her biggest smile.

Soon they were all hungry. Ben and Aunty Cass got the picnic ready.

"I've brought something, too," said Maya. She took out the sandwiches her mom had made.

"Thanks!" said Leroy, tucking in.

Maya smiled.

After lunch they went to the beach. It was full of rock pools.

"I've found a crab!" called Maya. Everyone came to look.

"First prize goes to Maya!" Ben said, laughing. He handed her a piece of wet seaweed.

"Ughh!" Maya giggled .

They played on the beach all afternoon. First they played frisbee. Then they made a sandcastle. Maya and Ben stuck shells round the sides. Donna and Leroy built the moat.

At last Aunty Cass came up.

"That's a great castle," she said. "But it needs a flag." She stuck a feather in the top.

"My mom always does that!" said Maya. Suddenly she missed her mom very much.

It was time to go back to the tent. Aunty Cass held out her hand. "Come along, Maya," she said kindly.

"I don't want to hold hands," grumbled Maya.

Aunty Cass gave Maya a funny look.

At the tent, everyone helped with the barbecue.

"I'm cold!" complained Maya. She watched Donna searching through the rucksacks.

"Has anyone seen the baked beans?" asked Donna.

"That's mine! Now it's all messed up," moaned Maya. And she snatched her rucksack away.

Donna stared at her.

What's wrong with Maya? How do you think the others feel?

Ben was sorting out the sleeping-bags.

"Give us a hand!" he said.

He threw Maya her sleeping-bag. But she let it fall on the ground.

"It's all dirty now!" screeched Maya.

"It wasn't my fault!" said Ben.

"You old misery!" said Donna to Maya. "Miserable Maya, that's you!"

Aunty Cass heard it all. "Come on, no arguments!" she said loudly.

"Maya's in a mood!" said Ben and Donna together.

Maya's lip wobbled.

"Come and have a chat," said Aunty Cass quickly, and she helped Maya out of the tent.

"Everything's horrible," sobbed Maya. "The others are calling me names."

Aunty Cass put her arm round Maya.

"They're all mixed up, that's all," she said. "First you were happy. Now you're cross. They don't understand."

"Neither do I," said Maya.

"I think you're missing your mom," said Aunty Cass. "You're a bit worried about being here without her. It's put you in a bad mood."

"I can't help it!" Maya sniffed.

"It's OK," said Aunty Cass. "Stay and chat with me. And when you feel better, go back to the others."

Maya felt much better already.

"I like talking to you," she said, squeezing her aunt's hand. "It's a bit like talking to my mom."

How did Aunty Cass help?

Feeling like Maya

Maya was happy at the beach. She got on well with Donna, Leroy and Ben. Then she began to miss her mom. It put her in a bad mood. And suddenly everything seemed to upset her. She started to moan.

All mixed up

Changing from one mood to another can be confusing. First you're happy, then you're sad. And sometimes it's hard to understand why. The mood just takes you over. It's hard for other people, too. They don't like it. Moaners spoil everyone's fun.

12

Being moody

If your moods are a problem, you can do something about it. Remember that no one is cheerful all of the time. It's OK to feel bad sometimes. But moaning doesn't help. Talking does.

Think about it

Read the stories in this book. Think about the people in them. Do you feel like them sometimes? Next time a mood takes you by surprise, think what you'll do. Who will you talk to?

13

Jason's story

"Put that light out, Jason!" called Jason's dad for the third time. It was very late. But Jason still hadn't finished reading.

"OK Dad!" Jason answered. He switched off his lamp. Then, very quietly, he slipped out of bed. He crept to his cupboard and opened a drawer. Jason found his flashlight and hurried back to bed.

Jason was sleepy. He had school tomorrow. He knew he should put his book down. But he was right in the middle of a pirate story. Jason clicked on his flashlight. He snuggled down under the covers and quickly turned another page.

Jason read on and on.

The next day Jason didn't hear his alarm.

"Wake up!" called Jason's mom loudly.

"Mmmm!" went Jason from under his covers.

Jason didn't have time for breakfast. He ran all the way to school. But he was still late. Jason was in a bad mood.

All morning Jason yawned. It was hot in the classroom. And his eyes kept closing.

"Wake up!" said Jason's friend Sam, giggling.

But Jason didn't think it was funny.

After lunch, Jason's class did their project. Jason and Sam were working together. They were making a book. It was all about the rainforest.

"You draw the snake – and I'll do the parrot," said Sam.

Jason sighed. He didn't want to do anything. He scribbled round and round on the paper.

"Hey! You're spoiling it!" said Sam.

"Shut up!" snapped Jason. He threw down his pencil.

How do you think Sam feels?

At last it was time to go home. Jason's friends were going to the park.

"Let's have a kick around!" said Charlie. He headed the ball to Jason.

Jason missed the ball. But he didn't go after it. He couldn't be bothered.

"What's the matter?" asked Charlie.

"He's in a bad mood," said Sam.

Sam and the others ran into the park. They didn't wait for Jason, and Jason didn't feel like catching up. He wanted to go home.

At home, Jason kicked off his shoes. His little brother Tom was waiting for him.

"Come and play with me!" said Tom.

"Get lost!" said Jason.

Tom ran out of the room. Jason could hear him crying in the kitchen.

Just then, Jason's mom came in. She was frowning.

"Why were you nasty to Tom?" she asked.

"I've had a bad day," said Jason. "I'm in a bad mood."

"That's not Tom's fault," said Jason's mom.

At bedtime, Jason's dad came for a chat.

"I've heard about your bad mood," he said.

"Today's been awful," said Jason. "I've been mean to everyone."

"Do you know why?" asked his dad.

"Because I'm tired," said Jason. "I'm too tired to be friendly."

Do you know what Jason means? Have you ever felt like Jason?

Jason gave a big sigh. "Sam went off – and I made Tom cry," he said. "Everyone hates me now!"

"They don't!" His dad smiled. "But I can think of two things to help. The first is to tell everyone you're sorry."

Jason nodded. He wriggled down in the bed.

"And the second is – to get some early nights," said his dad.

But Jason was already fast asleep.

Feeling like Jason

Do you like to stay up late, like Jason? Do you keep getting told to put out the light? It might seem that adults are spoiling your fun. But rest is important for everyone. Tiredness makes us snappy. It can put us in a bad mood. It can make us mean to our friends.

Think of others

What puts you in a bad mood? You may be tired, like Jason, worried or unwell. Whatever the reason, remember how other people feel. They may be hurt if you are nasty to them. Your bad mood isn't their fault. Try to say sorry to the people you've hurt. Then try talking about your feelings. Tell an adult you trust.

Beth's story

Beth was happy. It was the first sunny day for ages. She was going to the city farm with her mom.

"Do you think there'll be lambs yet?" asked Beth.

"I imagine so," said Beth's mom. "Now, wear your warm coat – it's still cold outside."

Beth found her scarf and gloves. Then she put on her heavy boots. She hummed a tune to herself. Beth loved the farm at this time of year. There might even be a newborn calf.

It was a long way to the farm. Beth's mom walked fast, but Beth went running on ahead. She couldn't wait.

"Hold on!" laughed Beth's mom. "We must stop at the store first. I need to get a few things."

Beth wasn't expecting that.

Beth hated going to the store. This big supermarket was worst of all. The lights were too bright. And the music was awful! Beth followed her mom around slowly.

"Let's do this on the way home," said Beth.

"We won't feel like it then," said her mom.

"I don't feel like it now," Beth said.

There was a long line at the checkout. Beth pulled off her scarf. "I'm boiling," she grumbled.

Outside, Beth's mom saw a friend.

"Not now!" wailed Beth. But Beth's mom was saying hello.

Beth waited. She stood on one foot, then on the other. She picked at a hole in her glove.

Beth's mom didn't talk for long. Soon she called out, "City Farm, here we come!"
But Beth didn't smile.

How do you think Beth is feeling?

24

At last, Beth and her mom reached the farm. It was very noisy. There were ducks quacking and geese hissing. A big rooster shouted, "Cock-a-doodle-doo!"

"He's saying Good Morning!" Beth's mom laughed. But Beth only frowned.

Then they heard some squeals.

"Look, Beth – piglets!" called her mom.

But Beth wouldn't look. And she wouldn't say a word.

What's the matter with Beth?

There was a crowd of children in the barn. And lots of woolly lambs. "We're feeding the lambs," called the farmer. "Come and join in!"

Beth turned away. A little girl held out a bottle of milk. Beth saw a lamb suck at it hard.

"Ooh! He's greedy!" giggled the girl.

Beth stood in the corner of the barn. She pushed her hands deep into her pockets. She pretended she wasn't watching.

Beth's mom came over. Beth wouldn't look at her.

"Let's go and see the goats!" said Beth's mom. "Or would you like lunch?" Beth sighed and shrugged.

"I'm fed up with this!" said Beth's mom crossly. "We might as well go home!"

"OK," said Beth, pretending she didn't care.

Do you think Beth really wants to go home? How do you think her mom feels?

At home, Beth went to her room. She tried to read a book, but she kept thinking about the farm. Beth felt sad.

After a while, Beth's mom came in.

"Have you finished sulking yet?" asked Beth's mom.

"Yes," said Beth quietly. "I'm sorry."

"I know you didn't like shopping," her mom went on. "But we all have to do things we don't like sometimes. And sulking doesn't help, does it?"

"It spoils everything!" said Beth.

Is Beth's mom right?

Beth's mom sat down next to her.

"I wanted to feed the lambs really," said Beth. "I didn't really want to be left out."

"I know," said her mom. She put her arm round Beth. "Shall we go to the farm again next week?"

"Yes, please!" said Beth. "I promise I won't get in a bad mood."

"OK," smiled her mom. "And if we need to go shopping, I promise I'll warn you first!"

"OK," said Beth, laughing.

Feeling like Beth

Have you ever been moody, like Beth? Have you ever felt sorry for yourself. and sulked? When you're sulking, you want others to feel sorry for you, too. The trouble is, it only drives them away or makes them angry.

Stopping sulks

Once a sulk starts, it quickly grows. It soon becomes hard to think of anything else. And, as Beth found out, sulking can spoil things. If you're feeling sulky, try not to let the feelings grow. Try to think of all the ways in which you are lucky. Remember, the longer you sulk the more you'll be missing out.

Managing moods

It's hard to cope with moods, even when you're an adult. But bad moods can spoil your own fun and other people's. Learning to manage your moods is part of growing up. And it does get easier – with practice.

Thinking about moods

Think about the stories in this book. Maya moaned, Jason snapped and Beth sulked. And they each learned something about their moods. What have you learned about moods – and about managing them?